THE HAPPY
AND HIS DUMP TRUCK

By MIRYAM
Illustrated by TIBOR GERGELY

GOLDEN PRESS • NEW YORK
Western Publishing Company, Inc., Racine, Wisconsin

ONCE UPON A TIME there was
a man who had a dump truck.
Every time he saw a friend, he waved
his hand and tipped the dumper.

One day he was riding in his dump truck when he passed a pig standing by the side of the road.

Before the man had a chance to tip his dumper,
the pig climbed right into the back of the truck.

A little farther down the road, the man saw
a friend. He waved his hand and tipped the dumper.

"Whee!" said the pig as he slid down to the bottom of the dumper. "This is fun!"

Soon they came to a farm. A cat, a rooster, a hen, a duck, and a dog were standing by the fence.

"Maybe they would like to ride with the pig,"
thought the man. So he stopped the truck
and tipped the dumper.

The hen and the rooster climbed into the truck. The duck, the dog, and the cat climbed into the truck. And the pig climbed back into the truck, too.

Then off they went!
When they passed the farmer,
all the animals waved to him.

The happy man waved to the farmer, too, and tipped the dumper.

The hen, the rooster, the duck,
the dog, the cat, and the pig all slid down
to the bottom of the dumper in a big heap!

The hen clucked.

The duck quacked.

The rooster crowed.

The dog barked.

The cat mewed.

And the pig gave a great big grunt.

The animals were having such a good time!
The man took them for a long ride.

When they got back to the farm, the man opened
the tail gate wide and tipped the dumper as far as
it would go.

The animals slid off the truck and onto the ground.
"What a fine sliding-board!" they all said.

The animals thanked the man for their ride.

"Cluck, cluck,"
clucked the hen.

"Cock-a-doodle-doo,"
crowed the rooster.

"Bow-wow,"
barked the dog.

"Quack, quack,"
quacked the duck.

"Meow, meow,"
mewed the cat.

And the pig gave a great big grunt. "Oink!"

The man waved his hand and tipped
the dumper again. Then he rode off in his truck,
singing a happy song.

Now, whenever the happy man rides past the farm, he gives the animals a ride in his dump truck.

And each animal always says "Thank you" in its own special way.